Jasper John Dooley
Left Behind

Jasper John Dooley
Left Behind

Written by Caroline Adderson

Illustrated by Ben Clanton

Jefferson Madison
Regional Library
Charlottesville, Virginia
Kids Can Press

3 0594 [0 2]

For Nana and Baba, who left us behind — C.A.

Kids Can Press acknowledges the financial support of the Government of Ontario, through the Ontario Media Development Corporation's Ontario Book Initiative; the Ontario Arts Council; the Canada Council for the Arts; and the Government of Canada, through the CBF, for our publishing activity.

Published in Canada by	Published in the U.S. by
Kids Can Press Ltd.	Kids Can Press Ltd
25 Dockside Drive	2250 Military Road
Toronto, ON M5A 0B5	Tonawanda, NY 14150

www.kidscanpress.com

Edited by Sheila Barry
Designed by Rachel Di Salle

This book is smyth sewn casebound.
Manufactured in Shen Zhen, Guang Dong, P.R. China, in 10/2012 by Printplus Limited

CM 13 0 9 8 7 6 5 4 3 2 1

Library and Archives Canada Cataloguing in Publication

Adderson, Caroline, 1963–
    Jasper John Dooley left behind / written by Caroline Adderson ; illustrated by Ben Clanton.

(Jasper John Dooley ; 2)
ISBN 978-1-55453-579-8 (bound)

    I. Clanton, Ben, 1988– II. Title. III. Series: Adderson, Caroline, 1963–. Jasper John Dooley ; 2.

PS8551.D3267L44 2013   jC813'.54   C2012-905447-X

Kids Can Press is a **LORUS**™ Entertainment company

Contents

Chapter 1

On Sunday morning Jasper John Dooley's Nan left on a holiday. Dad carried her big suitcase out of her apartment, and Mom carried Nan's small suitcase. Jasper took her purse. He rapped the jaws of the lion-head knocker that guarded Nan's place and said in a loud, liony voice, "Have a good trip, Nan!"

In his Jasper voice he asked, "Where are you going, anyway, Nan?"

"She's going on the trip of a lifetime," Dad said. "A cruise to Alaska."

"You mean on a boat?" Jasper said, going ahead to press the elevator button.

"On a ship," Nan said. "A huge ship."

"You're going on a ship trip?"

Everybody laughed. Then the elevator came, and they all got in. Jasper pressed "L" for lobby. "Why didn't you tell me about the ship?" he asked Nan.

"I did. I told you last Wednesday when you were over."

As they rode down, Nan told him about the ship again. "It has a swimming pool, a ballroom and ten restaurants. Imagine! Ten restaurants on one ship."

"Oh, right," Jasper said. "Now I remember. But I didn't know *you* were going on it. I thought it was something you saw on TV."

"She's really going," Mom said.

The elevator pinged and opened, and they all stepped out into the lobby. It looked like a jungle because of all the plants. A jungle with an elevator.

"It's going to be a wonderful week," Mom said.

"Week?" Jasper said. "Week? You're going to be back on Wednesday, aren't you, Nan?"

Every Wednesday after school Jasper went to Nan's to play Go Fish for jujubes.

Nan didn't answer. Maybe she hadn't heard him. Sometimes he had to get right up close for her to hear what he was saying. Then he thought of something else. Jasper liked going to the pool, and he really liked going to restaurants. He loved playing with balls — kicking them or trying to stand on them or balancing them on his head. He loved stuffing them up his shirt and saying, "Boy, I ate so so so so much."

"Can I go with you on the cruise, Nan?"

Everybody laughed again.

"What's so funny?" Jasper asked.

"It's an Elder Cruise, Jasper," Nan told him.

"What's that?"

"That," Dad said, "is eight hundred old people looking at icebergs."

"How old do you have to be to go on the cruise?" Jasper asked.

"About seventy-eight," Nan told him.

The car was parked out front. Dad put the suitcases in the trunk. When they were all in the car, they drove away from Nan's apartment, Nan and Jasper together in the backseat. "But you'll be back on Wednesday, right?" Jasper said.

"She'll be gone the whole week, Jasper," Mom said

from the front seat. "She'll be home next Monday."

"Nan! What about Go Fish? Nothing is as fun as playing Go Fish for jujubes!"

Nan sighed. "That is true, Jasper. That is true."

"Jasper," Dad said, "Nan has been planning this trip for a long time. If you keep talking like this, she won't want to leave."

"Don't leave!" Jasper cried. "Don't leave me behind!"

He grabbed Nan's hand and kissed the freckly brown spots on the back of it. Nan laughed and laughed. Then she asked for her purse, which was on the floor at Jasper's feet. He passed it to her, and she took a tissue out and dried her eyes. Jasper couldn't tell if they were sad tears or tears from laughing so hard. He took another tissue and pretended to dry his own tears with it. Pretending to cry made him feel all watery inside. For the rest of the drive, he held Nan's hand and sniffed it. Her perfumey smell was so nice.

Dad and Mom left Jasper and Nan on the dock while they went to drop off the suitcases and park the car. The ship was huge, just like Nan said. It looked like Nan's apartment building lying on its side, except it was white and it floated. Nan seemed worried when she saw how big it was. "Maybe you're right, Jasper. Maybe I'm too old to be taking a trip by myself."

Jasper looked around at the other people going up the ramp to the ship. Everybody had white hair except the people with gray hair. Many people walked with canes. Jasper pointed at one of the people with canes. "You're not so old, Nan. Look at him."

Nan smiled. "You always say the right thing, Jasper," and she kissed him seven times, once for every day of the cruise.

When Mom and Dad came back, Nan kissed them good-bye, too, and started up the ramp. Jasper waved and called, "Bye, Nan! Bye!" There were lots of people waving and calling good-bye at the same time. Jasper wanted to make sure Nan saw him so he took the tissue from his pocket and waved it. Just before Nan stepped onto the ship, she turned and blew kisses to Jasper.

They stayed a few more minutes after Nan got on the ship. Jasper waved with the tissue, then put it in his pocket in case any of Nan's kisses had got caught in it. He kept on waving with his hand, hoping Nan would see him through one of the cruise ship's tiny

windows. He waved so hard his arm almost fell off.
Then Nan was really, truly gone.

Back at the car, Jasper looked at himself in the side mirror. He saw four lipstick flowers on one cheek and three lipstick flowers on the other. Usually, lipstick flowers made him yuck. Today they made him sad.

"What about that ship, Jasper?" Dad asked.

Jasper said, "What ship?"

Later that night, after he went to bed, Jasper thought about his Wednesdays at Nan's. If Jasper won at Go Fish, which he almost always did, he got to take a jujube from the crystal bowl on the coffee table. He liked the red ones best, then the green, then the orange, then the yellow. He didn't like the black ones at all. But if Jasper let Nan win, which he did when he felt sorry for her, she always picked a black jujube. Black jujubes were her favorite. When all the jujubes were gone, they stopped playing cards.

Thinking about Wednesday made Jasper feel funny, not watery like he had in the car, but like all the air was seeping out of him. He called from his bed, "Mom! Mom! Mo-o-om!!!!"

Mom came. "What's the matter, Jasper?"

"I feel funny," Jasper said.

Mom laid her hand across his forehead. "You don't have a fever. Does your tummy hurt?"

"It doesn't hurt," Jasper said. "It just feels *pththth*."

"What's *pththth*?"

"It's like when my beach ball leaked. Do I look all flat?"

Mom sat on the bed. "You look like you miss Nan. But this week will go by so fast, Jasper John Dooley. Before you even know it, Nan will be back."

"Maybe I should stay home from school tomorrow and work on my lint collection," Jasper said.

Mom didn't think he should stay home. She said the best cure for missing somebody was just to get on with things. "I don't know if this will make you feel any better," she said, "but I bet Nan really misses you, too."

It did make him feel better. Nan was lying in her bed somewhere thinking about Wednesday, too. But where? Where was she lying?

"Where is Alaska, anyway?" Jasper asked.

Chapter 2

In the morning Jasper found a big book lying open where he usually ate his cereal. "Is this a new place mat?" he asked.

"It's an atlas," Dad said. "Mom told me you wanted to know where Alaska was." He showed Jasper on the map.

"Why is it a different color?"

"This huge orange country is Canada. Alaska is green because it's part of the United States, most of which is down here, under Canada," Dad said.

"How did Alaska get way up there?"

"That's too complicated to explain right now," Dad said. "Eat your cereal or you'll get the lates."

Jasper put his bowl of cereal over Alaska and began to eat. Nan was probably eating her cereal now, too, in one of the cruise ship's ten restaurants. She would be eating all by herself because she didn't know anybody. With Jasper's bowl right on top of her, she wouldn't feel so lonely. But what about all the other people way off by themselves?

"Does everybody in Alaska feel lonely?" he asked.

"What do you mean?"

"They're so far away."

"Everybody in Alaska is fine," Dad said, looking at his watch. "Are you done?"

Jasper finished his cereal and got to school on time.

It was Monday. On Monday after Star of the Week, they wrote stories, which Jasper liked. He liked writing long, long, long stories. If he wrote a long, long, long story, he got to go up to Ms. Tosh's desk and staple the pages together.

Jasper started a story about a little iceberg that got separated from the other icebergs. It was floating all alone in the ocean, feeling very sad. Finally, it found a place to dock, but it was still so far away from its family that it couldn't cheer up. Jasper wasn't even halfway down the page when he started to *pththth* again, so he ripped the story up.

He needed to write something that was the opposite of Nan so he wouldn't think about how she was away for a whole week and wasn't even coming back for Go Fish on Wednesday. The opposite of

Nan was all the things she didn't like. She really didn't like mice, or snakes, or loud noises, or wind messing up her hair. He couldn't think of anything to write about wind or loud noises. He'd already written three stories about Hammy, the little brown hamster in the cage at the back of the classroom. He decided to write about a snake.

His story was called "A Long, Long, Long Story by Jasper about a Snake." The snake in the story was six miles long. Jasper wrote in his biggest printing until the story was six pages. Then he put up his hand and asked to staple his pages together.

"Go ahead," Ms. Tosh said.

The stapler was one of Jasper's favorite things in the classroom, along with the cozy pillows in the Book Nook that you could hide under until somebody accidentally sat on you. And Hammy the hamster. Every Friday one of the kids got to take Hammy home for the weekend.

Jasper brought his story to Ms. Tosh's desk where there were even more things that he loved: the heart mug filled with spare pencils, the sticker shoebox, the electric pencil sharpener with a window that showed all the shavings inside.

Jasper piled his six pages on the desk. He took the stapler and *ker-chunked* one corner. Since the story was so long, six pages long, he *ker-chunked* the other corner, too. He put in four more staples along the side, just in case. *Ker-chunk. Ker-chunk. Ker-chunk. Ker-chunk.* Maybe a staple right in the middle would be good in case a big wind came up and blew through the classroom window and mixed the pages of everybody's stories together. Jasper gathered the pages off the desk and held them flat against his body. With the stapler open, he positioned it right in the middle of all the pages and *ker-chunked* hard.

"Owwwwww!!!!!!!"

All the kids looked up from their writing. Ms. Tosh came running. "Jasper! What have you done?"

All the kids said, "Ms. Tosh! Jasper stapled his story to himself!"

The nurse! He needed the nurse!

"Let's move slowly, Jasper," Ms. Tosh said. "Careful, careful."

All the way down the hall Jasper shuffled, his story stapled to his tummy.

"My goodness!" the nurse exclaimed when they got to the sickroom. She didn't wait for an explanation.

She put an arm around Jasper and led him over to the cot. He and his story lay down. Ms. Tosh wished him luck and went back to the class.

"What happened, Jasper?" the nurse asked.

"My Nan went away on a cruise. She went on a huge white ship with eight hundred old people. To look at icebergs."

"I see," the nurse said.

Jasper sniffed. "After that, I started going *pththth*. Because she left me. So I already had a hole in me. Now I have three!"

"Three?"

"A staple makes two holes," Jasper told her.

"Of course."

The nurse gave Jasper a tissue to wipe his eyes. Then she pointed at the ceiling and said, "What's that?" When Jasper looked up, she unstapled him. He didn't feel a thing. She asked him to lift his shirt, and there they were — two tiny holes in his tummy. The *pththth* hole from being left behind didn't show at all.

"Do they hurt?" the nurse asked as she dabbed the holes with a wet cotton ball.

"No," Jasper told her.

The nurse handed him a box of different kinds and colors of Band-Aids.

"Take your time," she said, when Jasper couldn't make up his mind which Band-Aid to choose. "I'm just going to walk around the school and see if anybody else has stapled himself."

After she left, Jasper took all the Band-Aids out of the box and held each one against his tummy. It was as much fun as picking a sticker from the shoebox on

Ms. Tosh's desk. In the end, he chose a Band-Aid the color of a green caterpillar.

"Good choice," the nurse said when she came back.

She put the Band-Aid on Jasper, then asked to read the story that he'd stapled to himself. She laughed and laughed. Jasper felt pleased that he'd written such a funny story. Then the bell rang for recess, and he sat up on the cot.

"Are you sure you're okay?" the nurse asked.

"Yes!"

Jasper thanked her and ran outside and around the school until he found his friend Ori, who was in his class and lived across the alley and one house down. Ori was playing with some other kids. When Jasper lifted his shirt to show off his Band-Aid, everybody crowded around him. Everybody wanted to see.

He lifted his shirt again and again. He felt so so so so popular!

Nothing happened the rest of the day except when Jasper hid under the pillows in the Book Nook and Isabel sat on him and screamed. Jasper forgot all about stapling his story to his tummy until after school when he saw Mom waiting. As soon as Jasper saw her, he remembered that Nan was away and that he had three holes in himself. He clutched them and bent over.

"Are you okay?" Mom asked, hugging him. "Does it hurt?"

"I stapled my story to myself!"

"I know. The nurse phoned and told me."

"Why didn't you come and pick me up?" Jasper asked.

"She said you were fine. She said you were outside playing."

"I *was* fine," Jasper said. "But now I'm not. I'm wounded. I don't think I can walk."

"Here," Mom said, crouching down. Jasper got on her back.

They lived a block from the school. Out of all the kids in the class, Jasper lived the closest. Even so, out of all the kids, it was always Jasper who got the lates. Ori lived the second closest to the school, across the alley and one house down from Jasper, and he never got the lates. Usually they all walked home together — Jasper and Ori and Mom.

"You should see Jasper's Band-Aid," Ori told Jasper's mom. "It's green!"

"I can't wait," Mom said.

"Can Jasper come over?" Ori asked.

"I can't," Jasper said. "I'm wounded."

"The thing is," Ori said, "we have a whole bunch of wood left over from our renovation. My dad said I could build something."

"With a hammer?" Jasper asked.

"Yes."

"I didn't know you were renovating," Mom said.

"What *is* renovating?" Jasper asked.

"It's a new room in the basement," Ori told him.

"I'll be better tomorrow for sure," Jasper said, and Ori waved and went off down the alley to his own house.

At home, Jasper flopped down on the sofa and lifted his shirt for Mom. "Wow," she said. "I've never seen such a nice Band-Aid."

"I love it," Jasper told her. "I'm going to wear it for the rest of my life."

When Dad got home, Jasper told him the whole long story about why he was lying on the sofa. He told him about the iceberg, the stapler and the snake.

"Hold on, Jasper John," Dad said, and he sat on the sofa and put Jasper's head in his lap. "I'd like to hear more about that snake."

"Nan doesn't like snakes. This one was six miles long. His tail kept getting hurt. Cars ran over it. People stepped on it. Doors slammed on it."

"Ouch," Dad said. "Maybe you can answer this question. It's something I've wondered all my life. Where does the snake's body end and its tail start?"

"That's a good question," Jasper said.

"It's a hard question," Dad said.

Jasper thought a little, and then he smiled. "I know the answer."

"Really?"

"Yes," Jasper said. "A snake's tail actually starts at the end."

"Jasper John Dooley," Dad said. "You astound me."

"It hurt so much when the staple went in," Jasper said. "I have three holes now."

"Three holes?"

"Yes. One from Nan leaving. Two from when the staple went in."

"Ouch, ouch, ouch," Dad said.

Because of the three holes, Jasper got to lie on the sofa and watch cartoons until supper. He got to eat supper on the sofa, too.

At bedtime, Mom and Dad said, "We're quite sure you'll feel better in the morning, Jasper."

"What day is tomorrow?" Jasper asked.

"Tuesday."

"Good. I just don't want it to be Wednesday."

"David?" Jasper's mom said to his dad. "Did you tell him about Wednesday?"

"Not a word," Dad said.

"Wednesday is when I won't be able to play Go Fish for jujubes with Nan because she left me behind," Jasper said.

"Maybe you can play Go Fish for jujubes with the new baby-sitter," Dad said.

"David!" Mom said. She punched Dad on the arm.

"Ouch!"

Jasper sat up. "What baby-sitter? What baby-sitter are you talking about? Nan baby-sits me."

"Her name is Annie," Mom said.

"Annie? No! Yuck!"

Chapter 3

When Jasper woke the next day, it seemed as if Nan had been gone a long time. Jasper didn't know exactly how long. He wondered if she'd seen an iceberg yet. Then he remembered his holes and lifted his pajama top to look at the Band-Aid. Wounded! He lay back down.

Finally, Mom came to his room to find out why Jasper wasn't getting out of bed.

"I think I should stay home from school and work on my lint collection," Jasper said.

"Why?" Mom asked.

"I had a bad dream last night."

"Really?" Mom crossed her arms. She crossed her arms whenever she didn't believe what Jasper was saying. But Jasper really had had a scary dream last night after lying awake for a long time thinking so so so scary thoughts about Annie the baby-sitter.

"It was about the baby-sitter! She was so so so so old and instead of eyes — Mom? Instead of eyes?"

"What?"

"She had jujubes! One was green and one was yellow!"

Mom shivered. "That does sound horrible. But Annie isn't old at all. She's sixteen and probably has normal eyes."

Jasper crossed his arms. He didn't believe her.

"Listen, Jasper," Mom said. "I got an idea last night. Since you like writing so much, why don't you write down everything that happens to you this week? Write down what happens while Nan is gone. You can read it to her when she gets back. She'll want to know what she's missed."

"Nothing's happened," Jasper said.

"What are you talking about?" Mom said. "Yesterday you stapled your story to yourself."

"That's the other reason I should stay home and work on my lint collection," Jasper said, putting his hands over his Band-Aid.

"Okay. Fine. But if you stay home, you won't be able to go to Ori's after school and build."

Jasper got up right away because he really wanted to hammer.

As he was undressing, Jasper stopped to admire his caterpillar-colored Band-Aid again. Then he thought of something. "Mom!" he called. "Mom! What if my Band-Aid comes off while I'm at school? I'll start to *pththth*."

Mom came over and checked the Band-Aid. "It's on good and tight."

"I want another one. On top of this one. Just in case."

Mom went to the cupboard and came back with another Band-Aid, a plain one. "Are you sure you want to cover it? You like it so much."

"I don't want to," Jasper said. "I have to."

So she put a plain Band-Aid over the special one, which was too bad.

Jasper said, "Better make it two."

That day at school, after calendar and Star of the Week, they played What Am I? Jasper loved What Am I? Ms. Tosh waited for all the kids to settle at their tables, which took a long time, then she picked somebody to come to the front of the room. The person who was picked had to pretend to be something they were learning about. Everybody else had to guess what it was. They could be somebody in a story they were reading. They could be something from science or math. Jasper put up his hand for a turn, but Ms. Tosh picked Ori.

Ori went to the front of the room and curled up into a tiny ball.

"You're a baby!" Leon called.

Ori didn't move. He stayed curled up.

"You're a rock!" Jasper shouted.

Slowly, Ori began to uncurl and rise on his knees. Slowly, he spread his arms. Slowly, he lifted his smile to the ceiling.

"You're a seed!" Zoë screamed. "You're a seed growing into a plant!"

Last week all the kids had planted beans in little pots.

"Yes," Ori said, and he went back to his table.

"Very good, Ori," Ms. Tosh said.

Jasper put up his hand to go next. He waved it so hard his arm almost fell off. But the person who guessed right always got the next turn, so Ms. Tosh picked Zoë. As soon as Zoë put her feet together and her arms straight out at her sides, everybody shouted out at the same time. Everybody knew she was the plus sign. Because everybody had shouted out at once, Ms. Tosh didn't know who should take a turn. Jasper waved his hand again. Then he remembered he had a tissue in his pocket, the tissue he had waved to Nan with when she was going up the ramp of the ship. He took it out and fluttered it.

"Jasper," Ms. Tosh said.

Jasper was going to be Hammy. He was going to wriggle his nose and pretend to run on his wheel making the *Whirr! Whirr! Whirr!* sound. But as he marched up to the front of the class stuffing the tissue back in his pocket, he remembered Nan going up the ramp of the ship and stopping to blow him kisses. He had caught them in the tissue, but now Nan's kisses had fallen out all over the floor.

All day kids would walk on them with their dirty shoes. When a reading group met on the carpet, everybody would plop their bums right down on Nan's kisses.

"Jasper," Ms. Tosh said. "We're waiting."

Jasper stuck his hand under his shirt, over his three Band-Aids. Three Band-Aids weren't enough if Nan wasn't coming back by Wednesday to save him from Annie with the jujube eyes.

Through the window, he saw that it was raining. On the way to school, Dad had told Jasper that if it was raining on the cruise, Nan might not be able to see any icebergs. Then why had she even gone away? Why?

"Jasper?"

Jasper got down on his knees and curled up like Ori had, but not so tight.

"He's a seed, too," Isabel guessed.

"He's an egg."

"He's a ball."

"He's moving!"

Slowly, Jasper started to float across the carpet. He floated so slowly it was hard to see that he was moving at all.

"He's a bug!"

"Give us a hint," somebody asked, but Jasper didn't answer because icebergs can't talk.

"Jasper," Ms. Tosh said. "Can you give us a hint?"

"I'm white," Jasper said.

"He's a snowball!"

"He's a dirty tissue in a ball!"

Everybody laughed.

"Another hint!"

"I'm really big," Jasper said. "I'm really big, and I can't talk."

That was all Jasper would say. For a long time the kids kept trying to guess what Jasper was, but they were never right. Then Ms. Tosh asked everybody to take out their spelling books and copy the words for the week off the board. After everybody got busy, Ms. Tosh came over to the iceberg and crouched down with her warm hand on the iceberg's back. She whispered in the iceberg's ear, "Jasper? Is everything all right?" She rubbed his back and soon the iceberg didn't feel so cold anymore. He could stand up and go back to his table and spell.

Chapter 4

After school, it was still raining. Instead of going home, Jasper went to Ori's, across the alley and one house down. Ori showed him the mountain of wet wood in the backyard left over from the renovation. Jasper sniffed it. It smelled nice and woody. "Let's get started," he said.

"The thing is," Ori said, "my mom said we couldn't play outside if it's raining."

"Can we build inside?"

"That's the other thing," Ori said. "No. But anyway,

before we build, we need to make a plan. Never build anything without a plan. We didn't have one for our renovation. Then we had to pay somebody to come and do it right."

They went inside to eat a snack and make a plan. Ori's mom gave them celery sticks and cheese. Jasper ate the cheese but put his celery sticks behind his ears, like pencils. "Why are you putting celery behind your ears?" Ori asked.

"It helps me think," Jasper said, but really it was because he hated celery. Jasper adjusted the celery sticks. "That's better. Now I'll be able to make a plan."

"Let's build a fort," Ori said.

"Everybody builds a fort," Jasper said, and Ori agreed that a fort wasn't very original.

Jasper twiddled the sticks, thinking, until Ori

finished crunching his celery. Then Jasper took the sticks out from behind his ears and asked, "Can I see the renovation?"

They went down to the basement. There was a new wall with a white door in it where there hadn't been a door or a wall before. Ori opened the door. Inside was an empty room. The walls were white and so clean and bright the boys had to shield their eyes. "Can we go in?" Jasper asked.

"Just don't touch the walls," Ori said.

Standing in the middle of the room was like standing inside an iceberg. Or a — "Cruise ship," Jasper said.

"What?"

"Let's build a cruise ship."

By the time Jasper's mom came to pick him up,

Ori and Jasper had finished their plan, which turned out to be a drawing. They showed it to Jasper's mom. It was a drawing of a ship as big as an apartment building lying on its side. It was so big it had a swimming pool and a ballroom. It had ten different restaurants. You couldn't see the pool or the ballroom or the restaurants because they were inside the ship. "There's a Ping-Pong room, too," Jasper said. "And you can ride your bike inside. One of the restaurants only sells popcorn. We're going to drive our ship out into the ocean and meet Nan there and bring her back with us."

"That's terrific," Jasper's mom said. "I can't wait until it's finished."

"The thing is," Ori said, "you won't be able to go on it."

"Only people who are old or young will be allowed on this ship," Jasper told her. "It's an Older–Younger cruise ship. No Middle people. Sorry."

Ori said, "We're going to start building tomorrow. If it isn't raining. Jasper will have to come back. He'll have to come back every day."

"I have to," Jasper told Mom. "I never got to hammer."

"That's fine," Mom said.

They headed home across the alley.

"Is it going to rain tomorrow?" Jasper asked on the way.

"I don't know," Mom said.

"I hope not," Jasper said. "I want to start building." Then he asked, "Do you think it's raining on the cruise?"

"It might be."

"Is it the same rain?" Jasper asked.

"It's very similar," Mom said.

Jasper said, "Nan went all the way to Alaska to see icebergs. If it's raining, she won't see any. And there was an iceberg around here today. She didn't have to go away at all."

"I've never seen an iceberg around here."

"You're probably not looking for one."

They went up the steps to the porch. Mom shook out her wet umbrella and left it outside. "Let's hope it's not raining where she is," she said.

"But then she'll be missing all this nice rain!" Jasper said.

"Like you said, it might be raining in Alaska, too."

"But it's not the *same* rain," Jasper said. "It's only *similar*."

Jasper got an idea. "I'm going to put out some containers to catch the rain. So Nan will have some when she gets back. And! I almost forgot! I need more Band-Aids."

"You have three on already," Mom said.

"I need more. Today at school? In the middle of What Am I? I started to *pthththt*."

Mom sighed loudly and went and got the box. Jasper lifted his shirt for her to put more Band-Aids around the edges of the other three Band-Aids. Four more Band-Aids. Then the box was empty. "Oh, no!" Jasper cried.

"We'll get more tomorrow. On our way back from Nan's."

"Is Nan coming home tomorrow?" Jasper asked.

"No. We have to water her plants. Tomorrow is only Wednesday."

"Wednesday?" Jasper took off, running through the house, waving his arms and yelling, "Not Wednesday! Not Annie! No jujube eyes! No!"

Chapter 5

As soon as Jasper woke on Wednesday morning, he checked his Band-Aids to make sure they hadn't come off in the night. All seven Band-Aids were still there. Too bad the nicest one was under all the others.

Nothing happened at school except that Jasper traded his cookie at lunch for two of Ori's celery sticks and put them behind his ears during math. When Ms. Tosh asked him what he was doing with celery behind his ears, he showed her how twiddling

the sticks helped him think of the right answer.
Ms. Tosh made him throw the celery in the garbage.
On the way to the garbage can, Jasper passed her
desk and stopped to sharpen one of the celery sticks
in the electric pencil sharpener with the window.

"Stop that right now, Jasper John!" Ms. Tosh said.

Other than that, nothing happened.

It wasn't raining, so after school Jasper went across
the alley and one house down to Ori's to start work
on the cruise ship.

Ori taped the plan on the side of the garage above
the mountain of wood. The boys stood with their
hands on their hips, studying it. That was how you
were supposed to stand when you looked at plans,
Ori said. They decided to start by laying out the
wood in the outline of the cruise ship. Each took

one end of a piece of wood and laid it in the grass. First they laid out a huge rectangle. Then they added a triangle at the top. They stood inside the outline to make sure it was big enough. They lay down in it.

"Nice," Jasper said.

Ori sneezed. "The thing is, I'm allergic to grass."

"That won't be a problem once the ship is in the water," Jasper said. He hopped up. "Okay. Let's hammer."

The tools were in the garage. Ori brought out a hammer and a coffee can full of nails. "Is there only one hammer?" Jasper asked.

"No," Ori said. "There's more than one hammer."

Jasper looked at Ori. The sun was shining red through his ears where they stuck out. "Aren't you going to hammer?" Jasper asked him.

"No," Ori said. "The thing is? When my dad was working on the renovation? Before we had to pay somebody to come and do it right? He hit his thumb with the hammer. It turned black and fell off."

"His thumb fell off?"

"It could have," Ori said.

Jasper grabbed the hammer. "I'm not scared."

So Ori climbed on top of the mountain of wood and watched Jasper hammer the outline of the cruise ship together. "I know! I can be the boss!" Ori said. He started calling, "Faster! Faster!"

"Did you know," Jasper asked, "that a snake's tail actually starts at the end?"

"Faster!" Ori shouted.

Jasper didn't hit himself with the hammer. He didn't hit many nails, either. For some reason he kept missing them. The nails were probably scooting out of the way when they saw the hammer coming down on their heads, scooting so fast Jasper couldn't even see them move. When Mom called from across the alley and one house down, the cruise ship wasn't even close to being done.

"Jasper John! We're going now!"

"We'll have to work really hard tomorrow," Jasper told Ori.

"Harder and *faster*!" Ori said.

Chapter 6

Jasper and Mom walked over to Nan's apartment to water the plants. On the way, Jasper said, "I have a feeling Nan is back."

"You'd like her to be back, I know," Mom said. "But she's not. She'll be gone the whole week."

"Maybe she never really went away."

"You saw her get on the ship," Mom said.

"Maybe she went out the back door and came home when we weren't looking."

"I don't think there is a back door on a ship."

"Ori and I are going to have one on the cruise ship we're making," Jasper decided.

Mom used Nan's key to get in the jungley lobby of the apartment building.

"Maybe she came home early," Jasper said, "because she missed me and doesn't want Annie with the jujube eyes to baby-sit me."

"I'm sure she misses you," Mom said. "But if she came back early, I think she would have called us."

"She wanted it to be a surprise," Jasper said.

Mom pressed the button for the elevator. "Hey!" Jasper said. "That's my job!"

The elevator came, and Jasper and Mom got in. Jasper pressed the button for Nan's floor. As soon as the doors closed again, he made a horrible face in the mirrored wall of the elevator. He and Nan always made horrible faces when they rode up to her apartment. They had contests to see who made the most horriblest face. Jasper always won except when Nan used her glasses. She pushed the frames of her glasses into her eye sockets. It made her eyes stretch down. She looked so so so so so so ugly! Jasper couldn't even tell it was Nan anymore. She looked more like Annie!

"Let's make horrible faces in the mirror," Jasper said.

Mom stuck out her tongue. It wasn't horrible at all.

"Never mind," Jasper said.

When the elevator arrived on the twenty-third floor, even before it opened, Jasper pressed the lobby button. "Let's go again."

"Why?" Mom asked.

"Because that's what I do with Nan. We ride up and down."

"Only once," Mom said as the elevator began to go down again.

"Also," Jasper said, "it will give Nan more time to hide."

"To hide?" Mom asked.

"So she can jump out and surprise us. Because she came home early."

They went down and up, down and up. Then Mom said, "That's enough, Jasper."

"I go up and down a lot more times than that with Nan."

"I'm starting to feel sick. Also, Dad and I are going out tonight, remember?"

"Jujube Annie!" Jasper cried. "Yuck!"

Outside Nan's apartment, Jasper clacked the lion's jaw against the door. *Clack! Clack! Clack!* "Come out, come out, wherever you are!" he called.

Mom unlocked the door. It smelled funny inside. Usually, the apartment smelled of cooking and Nan's perfume. Now it smelled like stale socks. Jasper called out, "Hello, Nan!" He slipped off his shoes and ran around the apartment looking for Nan in the closets and under the beds. In the spare bedroom was a trunk of old clothes that Jasper and Nan used for playing Dress Up Nan. That's where she was! Jasper crept over to the trunk and flung it open.

She wasn't in the trunk. So Nan really was still in Alaska.

Jasper started to *pththth*. Quickly, he stuck his nose right down into the trunk. Smelling the nice old clothes smell made him feel a little better. He felt even better when he climbed into the trunk and shut the lid.

After a minute, Jasper got the idea to scare Mom. He called, "Mom! Mom!" He waited a bit before calling again, louder. "MOM!"

The nice smell in the trunk got stronger. Soon it wasn't so nice because it was hard to breathe. Gasping, Jasper pushed the lid open and sat up.

Mom was standing in the bedroom door holding a watering can.

"Why didn't you help me?" Jasper asked.

"I only just heard you," Mom said. "What are you doing?"

"I was suffocating."

"Oh, Jasper," Mom said. "I'm just going to water the

plants. Then we're going."

"Nan would never let me suffocate," Jasper told her.

Jasper climbed out of the trunk. The clothes in it
were from when Nan was young. Though a lot of
them didn't fit her anymore, she could still wear the
fancy dressing gowns and the gold shoes and jewelry.
On Wednesdays, after she put on the things Jasper
chose for her, they went to Nan's bedroom where
she had a table with a special mirror with lights all
around it. Jasper combed Nan's hair and pinked her
lips and cheeks with pink stuff. He sprayed her with
lots and lots and lots of perfume. Then Nan and
Jasper went to the living room to play Go Fish for
jujubes.

But not this Wednesday.

Mom was in the living room watering the plants

on the windowsill when Jasper came in wearing
Nan's gold dress and fur shawl with little paws
hanging off it and many, many plastic necklaces.

"Oh!" Mom said. "Is this what you do on Wednesdays with Nan?"

"No. Usually Nan dresses up. But she's not here. She left me behind."

"Well, you look very nice." She went to water the African violet on the bookshelf. Jasper teetered on Nan's high-heeled shoes over to the coffee table where the cards and the jujubes were. He took the cards out of the box and shuffled them, which he did by spreading them out on the table and smearing them around. When Mom saw him, she said, "Do you want to play a hand before we go?"

"Okay," Jasper said.

Mom didn't know how! He tried to explain the rules to her, but she didn't seem to understand. "You say, 'Give me your aces!' But you have to say it that way. Like you're so so mad. And if I don't have any aces, I'll shout, 'Go fish, HA HA HA!' And you have to scream."

"I have to?"

"Yes. That's how you play Go Fish," Jasper said. He dealt out the cards. It was hard to do wearing all the plastic necklaces. His hand kept getting tangled up. Also, the fur shawl was itching his neck. While he was dealing and scratching and untangling his hand, Mom took the lid off the crystal bowl and popped a yellow jujube into her mouth.

"No!" Jasper shouted, too late.

"What?" Mom said.

"You only get the jujubes when you win the hand! And I always get the colored ones!"

"Fine. I'll take a black one."

She popped another one in her mouth!

"No!" Jasper shouted, lunging and clapping his hand over the bowl. It flew off the coffee table and landed on the carpet. Jujubes scattered everywhere.

"Jasper John Dooley," Mom said. "What is the *matter* with you?"

"I'm saving those for when Nan gets back. Nan gets the black ones. Because we are perfect companions. A companion is a friend."

"I know that, sweetheart," Mom said.

"Do you know why we're perfect companions?"

"Because she's your Nan and you're her favorite and only grandson?" Mom said.

"No! Because, together, we eat all the jujubes in the bowl!"

Then Mom made him get down on his hands and knees and pick all the jujubes off the floor.

That night Jasper was the only one eating because Mom and Dad were going to a restaurant. He sat in the kitchen all by himself with his macaroni while Dad showered and Mom dressed. After a few minutes, Jasper started to feel like that little iceberg in the story he had ripped up. He started to *pththth,* so he went to his mom and dad's room. Mom was sitting at her desk painting her fingernails.

"Can I do that?" Jasper asked.

"That's nice of you to offer, Jasper," Mom said. "But painting nails isn't for little boys."

"Nan lets me help her with her makeup," Jasper said.

"Really?" Mom said. "I'd rather you didn't help with my nails. It's sort of important to stay in the lines."

"Can I comb your hair?"

Mom blinked at Jasper. "Okay."

Jasper ran to the bathroom to get Mom's comb. It was hard to find in the big steam cloud that filled the whole room. "Gail! Is there any dandruff shampoo?" Dad asked from behind the shower curtain.

Mom was blowing on her nails when Jasper came up behind her and started combing. "Ow!" she said, bringing her hand up to her head. "Jasper John! What are you doing?"

Jasper said, "Combing your hair."

"You snuck up. You startled me. Now I've got hair marks on my nails. I'll have to put on another coat."

"I can do that for you," Jasper said.

She didn't even answer. Dad came in the room with a towel wrapped around his waist. Mom said, "David, do I have nail polish in my hair?"

So Jasper went back to the kitchen. He got an idea right away. He could eat his macaroni with the comb instead of the fork! But just as he was about to scoop some up, he thought, "I better not."

Instead he went outside on the deck and checked the yogurt containers he had left out for Nan. A little bit of rain filled the bottom of each one. He snapped the lids on and brought them into the kitchen and put them in the fridge where they would stay fresh. Then he got some more empty containers from the cupboard and set them out on the deck railing in case it rained again. Even if it didn't rain, Nan wouldn't want to miss all the nice air Jasper was breathing.

A little while later the doorbell rang. Mom called, "Jasper, can you get that?" Only then did Jasper remember that Jujube-Eye Annie was coming. He ran to Mom and Dad's bedroom where Mom was pulling her dress over her head and Dad was tying his tie.

"Please take me with you! Please don't leave me behind with Annie!"

Chapter 7

Jasper opened the front door wearing his best, unfriendliest frown. It was Annie. She wasn't old, and her eyes looked normal, just like Mom said. But there was something different about her. Jasper noticed right away.

"Oh!" he said.

Mom came to the door zippering her dress. She said, "Hello. You must be — Oh!"

Then Dad came with his best, friendliest smile. "Hel — Oh!"

Jasper said to Annie, "You have a ring in your nose."

Mom had told Jasper that Annie baby-sat lots of the kids in the neighborhood. She had told Jasper that all the mothers loved Annie. One of them had given Jasper's mom Annie's phone number. But Mom hadn't said anything to Jasper about the ring in Annie's nose. From the look on Mom's face, Jasper knew no one had told Mom either.

Annie smiled and shook Mom and Dad's hands. She shook Jasper's hand, too. "Nice to meet you. I think we're going to have a lot of fun, Jasper," she said.

"Don't worry about anything," she told Mom and Dad.

Mom already looked worried. She looked so so worried, but Dad made her put on her coat and go.

After Mom and Dad left, Jasper told Annie,

"Usually my Nan baby-sits me. She doesn't have a ring in her nose."

"Where is she tonight?" Annie asked.

"On a cruise."

Jasper told Annie about the ship. He told her about the swimming pool and the ballroom and the ten restaurants. "Nan wants to see icebergs," he said. "She's never left me behind before."

"You must miss her," Annie said.

"I do!" Jasper said.

"So, how about we go on a cruise, too?" said Annie. "Then you won't miss her so much."

Jasper said, "I had exactly the same idea! I'm building a cruise ship in my friend Ori's backyard, across the alley and one house down."

"It will take quite a while to build a huge cruise

ship," Annie said. "I was thinking about going tonight."

"Tonight?" Jasper asked. "How?"

"First we have to set up the restaurants. How many did you say?"

"Ten."

"How about four?"

Jasper said, "Okay."

They put cookies in the living room, grapes in Mom and Dad's room, milk in the kitchen, and ice cream in the dining room. Jasper told her that one of the restaurants in his and Ori's cruise ship was only going to sell popcorn.

"Do you have any popcorn?" Annie asked.

They checked the cupboard. They didn't.

"Then why don't we start with ice cream?" Annie said.

"Aren't you going to make me eat my fruit first?" Jasper asked.

"Do you want the ice cream to melt?"

"No!" Jasper said and sped ahead.

After they finished the ice cream, Annie said she felt like a swim in the pool. "How about you, Jasper?"

Jasper felt like swimming, too. On the way to the pool, they stopped off in the living room to eat the cookies.

Annie filled the tub, and Jasper started to undress. As soon as he pulled his shirt over his head, Annie gasped. "Nobody told me you had your appendix out!"

"What's a pendix?" Jasper asked.

"It's inside you." Annie pointed to his Band-Aids. "Did you have an operation?"

"No. That's where I stapled my story to myself."

"Say that again."

"It's a long story," Jasper said.

He told Annie about the snake. He told her how

nice the first Band-Aid was and how Mom had put two more Band-Aids over it the next day but still he *pthththed* at school and needed more Band-Aids over those ones.

"How many does that make?" Annie asked.

"Twelve," Jasper told her. "But that first one was so nice."

"And how does the snake fit in?" she asked.

"That was the story. He was so long people kept stepping on his tail," Jasper said. "Most people don't know where a snake's body ends and its tail starts."

"I guess I don't, either," Annie said.

"It starts at the end!"

"You're kidding," Annie said.

"No. And I think I need more Band-Aids before I go in the pool."

"Okey-dokey," Annie said.

Jasper showed her the cupboard where they kept the Band-Aids. It was a new, full box, so Annie put a lot more on. When he was all bandaged up, Jasper dove in the pool. He showed Annie the front glide that he had learned in swimming lessons. He showed her his back float and his roll-over.

Annie lay on the bathmat and pretended to be sun tanning.

Afterward, while Jasper was putting on his pajamas, the phone rang. He heard Annie say, "It's going great!" She called, "Jasper! Your mom wants to talk to you!"

Jasper came to the phone. "Are you all right?" Mom asked. She sounded worried.

"Yes!" Jasper said.

He was just a little bit hungry after all that swimming. Also, a big wet circle had appeared in the middle of his pajama top. After he got off the phone, he took off his top and pressed a towel against his Band-Aids while he and Annie ate grapes in Mom and Dad's room.

Then Jasper went around the house looking for balls. He found a baseball and a foam ball. He found his leaky beach ball. He put them on his bed. "This is the ballroom," he said, pulling a new pajama top over his head.

Annie laughed. "A ballroom is for dancing. But I like your idea better."

They played with all the balls. Jasper balanced on one, then stuck it up his top. "I ate so so so so much in all those restaurants," he said.

Annie knew how to juggle. She could juggle three different kinds of balls at once. Afterward, they went back to the first restaurant where Annie pretended to be a waitress serving him more ice cream. While they were eating, she asked if he wanted to dance, too.

"Does this ship have two ballrooms?" Jasper asked.

Annie said, "It could."

They went to the living room. Annie turned on the stereo and twiddled the dial until she found a station Mom and Dad never listened to. She turned it up LOUD. When she danced, her arms made circles in the air and her bottom wiggled as if her underpants were too tight. Jasper gave it a try. "This is fun!" he yelled.

He got an idea. "Hold on a sec."

Jasper ran to the kitchen and came back with a twist tie from the bread bag. He bent it into a ring and hung it from his nose. Annie laughed and laughed.

After dancing, they dropped into another restaurant for a drink of milk. Then Jasper brushed his teeth and went to bed.

"I think I need more Band-Aids," he told Annie. "These ones are still wet. They might come off in the night."

Annie put on more Band-Aids. Jasper fell asleep right away, even before Mom and Dad got home. "Oh, no," he thought as he was drifting off. "We forgot to look for icebergs!"

Chapter 8

The next morning at breakfast Mom asked about Annie. "Did you have fun?"

"Yes," Jasper said.

"What did you do?"

"Nothing." He got up from the table and started opening the kitchen drawers.

"What are you looking for?" Mom asked.

"Twist ties," Jasper said.

Dad checked the time. "Hurry, Jasper. Go get dressed or you'll get the lates."

And that's what happened. Jasper got the lates again, but not because he was looking for twist ties. He got the lates because of Dad.

While Jasper was dressing, Dad came into his room to hurry him up again. "Jasper!" he said. "Look at all those Band-Aids!"

Jasper looked at his tummy. Twenty-seven Band-Aids were holding the first one on. "You have to take those off," Dad said.

Jasper remembered the last time he'd hurt himself. Taking off the Band-Aid had hurt more than falling down and scraping his knee. It had hurt a lot more.

"No!" Jasper cried. "Taking them off will hurt more than getting stapled!"

"The trick is to rip them off."

"No! That's what you did the last time!"

"Fast. It won't hurt at all," Dad said, taking a step toward Jasper.

Jasper dropped down and slipped under Dad's legs. He ran right out of the room to Mom and Dad's room, where he hid behind the curtains, making himself so so flat. He'd *pthththed* so much since Nan went away he could be as flat as he wanted.

"Jasper!" Dad called. "You have to get going! Come on!"

Jasper didn't answer and Dad walked right past where he was hiding. "If you let me take those Band-Aids off, I'll buy you something special!" he called.

Jasper wondered what Dad would buy him, but he kept his mouth shut.

"Your very own stapler?" Dad called.

Behind the curtain, Jasper shook his head.

⚓ ☸ ⚓

Nothing happened at school that day except that Jasper got the lates and then had to go to the principal's office for doing a Very Dangerous Thing at recess. Four kids did the Very Dangerous Thing — Jasper, Ori, Isabel and Zoë — but only Jasper got sent to Mrs. Kinoshita's office. Because the Very Dangerous Thing was his idea.

Mrs. Kinoshita folded her hands on top of her desk. She looked hard at Jasper in the big chair across from her. Jasper felt nervous. He always felt nervous when he sat in a chair too high for his feet to touch the ground.

"It's Very Dangerous to put things in your nose, Jasper," Mrs. Kinoshita said.

Jasper stretched his legs downward in the chair, but his feet still wouldn't touch. "Leon always puts things in his nose," he said.

"What does Leon put in his nose?" Mrs. Kinoshita asked.

"Fingers."

"A finger can't get stuck inside your nose."

"Sometimes it seems that Leon's finger will get stuck," Jasper said. "It seems like his whole hand is going to get stuck. You should see him."

"But a finger can't accidentally stab you in the brain the way a twist tie can."

"The twist ties were just hanging from our noses. What about celery behind the ears?" Jasper asked.

"Behind the ears is okay. In the ears? Never! Put nothing in your ears or nose, Jasper. It's Very

Dangerous. Particularly if you're horsing around."

"We were dancing," Jasper said.

"I saw you out the window," Mrs. Kinoshita said.

"Did you think our underwear was too tight?"

"No," Mrs. Kinoshita said. "I thought you were doing a Very Dangerous Thing, horsing around with twist ties in your nose."

"We weren't," Jasper insisted. "We were doing this." And he jumped out of the chair making circles with his arms and wiggling his bottom. He felt much more confident now that his feet were on the ground.

"Yes, I saw," Mrs. Kinoshita said. "Sit down."

Jasper said, "I prefer to stand."

Mrs. Kinoshita let him stand because she was almost finished talking to him. He only had to promise not to bring Very Dangerous Things like twist ties to school again and not to get other kids to do Very Dangerous Things, like put twist ties in their noses and horse around. Then she sent him back to his classroom.

On the way he stopped at the sickroom and knocked on the door so the nurse could check his Band-Aids. When she didn't answer, Jasper remembered that she only came to school one day a week. Luckily, it had been the day he stapled himself! He walked the rest of the way to the classroom backward because it would take longer, and he suspected they were doing math.

But they weren't! They were choosing who got to take Hammy home!

Every year Ms. Tosh's students got to name the real live little brown hamster in the cage at the back of the class. Last year he was Bob, but this year he was Hammy. Every Thursday Ms. Tosh drew a slip of paper out of a hat. On the slip of paper was the name of the kid who got to take Hammy home for the weekend.

Please, Jasper thought. *Please let it be my name today.*

More than half the class had already had a turn taking Hammy home. There weren't that many slips of paper left in the hat. All the kids who hadn't had a turn sat at their tables holding their breath. Jasper focused on his name. *Jasper.* He saw it written on the slip of paper. *Jasper.* He saw Ms. Tosh's hand reaching into the hat. *Jasper.* He saw her fingers touch the slip of paper that said *Jasper.* He saw all this, but his eyes were closed.

Jasper.

Jasper.

Jasper.

Then he saw Ms. Tosh read the name on the slip of

paper. *Jasper.* He saw Ms. Tosh frown because Jasper had just been in the principal's office for doing a Very Dangerous Thing at recess. *Please,* Jasper thought. *I'll never do it again. I'll never hang a twist tie from my nose and dance around!*

"Jasper."

Never again!

"Jasper?"

Somebody poked Jasper. He opened his eyes. Ms. Tosh was smiling at him and fluttering a slip of paper. The slip of paper that said *Jasper.*

Chapter 9

After school Mom was waiting for Jasper. "Mom!" Jasper shouted as he ran out to meet her. "Mom! It's my turn! It's my turn!"

"Your turn for what?"

Ori caught up and told her. "Tomorrow it's Jasper's turn to bring Hammy home for the weekend!"

Then Jasper remembered. He put his hands over the big lump of Band-Aids under his shirt. "Nan's not here! She won't get to meet Hammy!"

"If we ask nicely, Ms. Tosh might let you keep him an extra day."

"So she'll get to meet Hammy?"

"Hopefully," Mom said. "And you'll be so busy with Hammy and building your ship that you won't notice she's gone. Jasper will be right over," Mom told Ori. "I'm going to make you boys a snack."

Jasper was so excited about looking after Hammy and about Nan coming back on Monday that he almost forgot to bring in the yogurt containers before going over to Ori's. He went out on the deck and snapped the lids on. Four more yogurt containers of air. He put them in the fridge. Now there were four yogurt containers filled with rain and eight yogurt containers filled with air for Nan when she got home.

Mom packed the snack for him to share with Ori.

"You're going over there every day. I don't want you eating all their food," she said.

"I'm not eating all of it," Jasper said. "I'm putting some of it behind my ears."

Ori was already calling from across the alley and one house down. "Faster, Jasper! Faster!"

First they sat on the mountain of wood in Ori's backyard to eat their snack, which was apple slices and cheese bunnies. They counted out the cheese bunnies and divided them equally. One cheese bunny they broke in half. They didn't care about being fair with the apple slices.

Before Jasper had even finished his snack, Ori ordered him back to work.

"I'm not finished my cheese bunnies," Jasper complained.

"It doesn't matter. You have to get to work on time. Those people we had to pay to come and do our renovation? They always got the lates. Sometimes they never even came. My dad was so mad."

"I just want to finish my bunnies," Jasper said.

"We'll never get this cruise ship finished," Ori said.

"We might if you helped," Jasper said.

"I'm helping! I'm the boss!"

"I mean if we had two people hammering," Jasper said.

Ori started yelling. "I don't want to hammer! My dad hit his thumb with the hammer, and it turned black and almost fell off! Then we had to pay somebody!"

"My Nan is coming home on Monday!" Jasper yelled. "We have to get this ship done!"

"You'd better hurry," Ori said.

By then Jasper had finished his bunnies so he jumped down from the mountain of wood and picked up the hammer. He looked at the plan taped to the garage, then at the wood outline of the cruise ship that wasn't nearly nailed together yet.

"Faster!" Ori called.

Jasper crouched and took a nail from the coffee can. He tapped it part way into the piece of wood. So far so good. But when he raised the hammer high to drive the nail in, the same thing happened again. That sneaky nail jumped out of the way! Jasper kept at it, but he hardly ever hit the nail. Meanwhile, Ori kept on yelling, "Faster! Faster!"

Jasper threw down the hammer. "I've got an idea," he said. "Let's pay somebody to finish the ship. How much money do you have?"

Ori wasn't sure. He went inside to get his bank. He and Jasper emptied it on the mountain of wood and counted it out. There were eight dollars, seventeen pennies, three nickels and twelve dimes. "Wow," Jasper said, sweeping it all into the hem of his shirt. "This will be a big help."

"You're taking it all?" Ori asked.

"Yes. A cruise ship is expensive to build."

"The thing is," Ori said, "it's my wood. So you have to pay to build the ship."

Jasper let the money fall from his shirt into the grass. "No fair!"

He stormed off across the alley and one house down.

Chapter 10

Except at the very end, when Ms. Tosh gave Hammy to Jasper to take home, nothing happened at school the next day. Ori did whisper, "Faster!" when Jasper was trying to finish his math worksheet. And then Jasper wasn't fast enough and had to stay in at recess to get it done. Recess wasn't even enough time to finish the worksheet, not when Jasper spent half of it coloring his thumb black with a pen from Ms. Tosh's desk. And Jasper did march right up to Ori when he came in from recess and waggle his black thumb in

Ori's face. Ori staggered over to his desk and put his head down. When Ms. Tosh noticed, she asked if he was all right. Ori said he felt sick and was going to throw up, so Ms. Tosh sent him home, which was too bad because then Ori couldn't walk home with Jasper and his mom and Hammy.

But other than that, nothing happened.

At the end of the day, Ms. Tosh gave Mom a bag of hamster food and some wood chips for the bottom of the cage. She gave Jasper the cage. "Now, Jasper. Make sure you don't feed Hammy too much. Because — look at him."

"Hammy is hammy," Jasper said.

"He sure is," Ms. Tosh said. "Make sure he gets some exercise."

Mom said, "Ms. Tosh, Jasper's Nan has been away.

He misses her so much. Could he keep Hammy an extra day to surprise her when she gets back?"

Ms. Tosh said yes.

Jasper and Mom walked home with Hammy in his cage. Hammy looked out through the bars. He wiggled his nose. "He thinks he's on an airplane," Jasper said. He walked three steps before asking, "Can I please get my own hamster?"

"We'll see," Mom said. Then she asked where Ori was.

"He went home sick," Jasper said.

"That's too bad. I hope it's not catching. You've been over there a lot." Then she noticed Jasper's thumb. The ink he had colored it with had smeared all over his other fingers. "Jasper John Dooley, your hands are filthy!"

First thing when they got home, after he washed his hands, Jasper went around the house collecting cardboard tubes. He got tubes from paper towels. He got tubes from toilet paper. Mom let him unwind a roll of toilet paper just to get the tube out. Jasper put all the loose toilet paper in a box. The box was in the bathroom now. Mom said they had to use up that paper before they started a new roll.

When Dad came home he asked, "Why is there a box of loose toilet paper in the bathroom?"

Jasper ran with the cage to show him Hammy.

"Wow," Dad said. "That is one plump hamster."

After Jasper finished joining all the cardboard tubes together with tape, he took Hammy out of his cage to get some exercise. He put him in one end of the long, long tube and quickly crawled around to the other end. "Come on, Hammy! Come on, boy!" he called down the tube.

Hammy came. He came halfway. Then he got stuck. Luckily, it was easy to rip the tube open. Hammy didn't seem too bothered. He looked at Jasper and wiggled his nose.

That night Hammy slept in Jasper's room. In the middle of the night, Jasper woke to a sound. *Whirr! Whirr! Whirr!* It was Hammy running around the wheel in his cage. *Whirr! Whirr! Whirr!* Jasper put his pillow over his head.

Whirr! Whirr! Whirr!

He asked, "Hammy? Are you going to do that all night?"

Whirr! Whirr! Whirr!

He said, "Hammy! Pipe down!"

Whirr! Whirr! Whirr!

Jasper got out of bed and took the wheel out of the cage.

$$\text{⚓ ☸ ⚓}$$

When Jasper woke the next morning, he was worried. He was worried that there was a terrible disease you could get from looking at a black thumb. And he was worried that Hammy would be hammier on Tuesday because he had taken the exercise wheel out of Hammy's cage. Jasper was so so worried that he forgot to check if his Band-Aids had come off in the night.

He got up and put the wheel back. Hammy was sleeping in a ball in the corner of the cage. "There you go, Hammy," Jasper told him. "You can run all you want now."

Hammy kept on sleeping.

Jasper reached into the cage and put Hammy on the wheel. Hammy looked sleepily around. He wiggled his nose. When Jasper turned the wheel, Hammy climbed right off and went back to his little nest of wood shavings in the corner.

Jasper got an idea. He found some string and made a little leash, then lifted Hammy out of the cage and tied it around his tummy. Jasper didn't tie it very tightly. He didn't want to hurt Hammy. Then Jasper took Hammy to the kitchen where Mom was and set him on the floor.

"What are you doing with Hammy?" Mom asked.

"He's getting some exercise," Jasper told her at

exactly the moment Hammy slipped out of the leash and took off faster than he had ever run in his whole hammy life.

"Hammy!" Jasper screamed.

Mom and Dad and Jasper looked everywhere. They crawled on their hands and knees through the house, looking under the furniture and in every cupboard and closet. Jasper even checked his drawers.

"Hammy!" Mom called.

"Hammy!" Dad called.

"Come on, Hammy!" Jasper called. "Come on, boy!"

Dad found two sets of car keys that he had lost. Jasper found an armless action figure and some hockey cards. Mom found an earring and a lot of dirt. But they didn't find Hammy.

Hammy was really, truly gone.

"Don't worry," Dad told Jasper. "He's around here somewhere."

Mom said, "Let's lure him back with food. What special food do hamsters like to eat?"

"Macaroni?" Jasper said.

Mom said, "Let's start with cheese."

She went to the fridge for some cheese, which

she cut into tiny pieces. They made a cheese trail through the house. The trail started in the kitchen and went all the way to Jasper's room, ending right at Hammy's cage on the floor.

"Good," Dad said. "Now I think we should get out of the kitchen. If we're here, Hammy won't leave his hiding place."

Mom wanted to go to the garden center. She told Jasper, "Why don't you go over to Ori's and work on the ship?"

"No!" Jasper cried.

"You can come with me if you want. Or you can stay here and watch golf with Dad."

Jasper went down to the den with Dad, but the little ball rolling across the grass and ducking in the hole reminded him of Hammy escaping. Where had

Hammy gone? There wasn't a hole in the kitchen.

He pressed both hands over his Band-Aids. "I'm *pthththing* again. I need more Band-Aids."

"You need to take those Band-Aids off," Dad said.

"Never!" Jasper wailed.

"Shhh," Dad said. "You'll scare Hammy."

"If we don't get out of the house," Jasper said, "Hammy will never come back."

So Jasper and Dad went out for a walk. All their neighbors were outside enjoying the sunny Saturday. Dad waved and called to each of them, "Hamster on the loose!"

"I wish Nan was here," Jasper said. "She would know what to do."

"Nan would *not* know what to do," Dad said. "Nan would run screaming as fast as she could."

"What if Nan doesn't come back, either?" Jasper asked.

"Nan's coming back."

They walked past the alley, around the corner, then down Ori's street. Ori's dad was in the yard mowing the lawn. He shut the mower off when he saw them and came to shake hands with Dad across the fence. Jasper noticed that his thumbnail was black. It made him feel sick, and he clutched his Band-Aids again.

Ori's dad invited Jasper's dad inside to see the renovation. "Ori's in the backyard," he said, ruffling Jasper's hair. "Go see what trouble he's getting up to."

Jasper crept around the side of the house. Ori was working on the cruise ship by himself with his back turned. Jasper watched him tap a nail in until it could stand up by itself. Then he lifted the hammer with both hands. When he brought it down, he missed the nail completely. He wasn't even close.

"Ori," Jasper called.

Ori looked over his shoulder. As soon as he saw Jasper, he leapt up and ran and hid behind the mountain of wood.

"I washed my thumb," Jasper called, but Ori still wouldn't come out. Jasper felt a great gush of *pththth*. He buckled over, holding his Band-Aids tight. Then Dad called to him.

When Jasper and Dad got home again, they took off their shoes and tiptoed inside, down the hall and to the kitchen, without making any sound.

The cheese was gone, but Hammy wasn't in the cage.

"That is one smart hamster," Dad said.

Chapter 11

That night they made a trail of cracker crumbs. In the morning the crumbs were gone but Hammy was still on the loose. Dad looked in the fridge for something else hamsters might like to eat. He opened some containers. "Why are there so many empty containers in the fridge?" he asked.

"They're not empty!" Jasper said. "Close them! Quick! That's Nan's air!"

"How about raisins?" Mom said. "Everybody likes raisins."

After breakfast they made a trail of raisins. Then Mom suggested they all go out again. "Let's go to the library. Let's get some advice."

They rode their bikes to the library and locked them in the rack out front. Inside, they went over to the desk where the librarian sat like a hen on a nest. Jasper asked her, "Do you have a book called *How to Be Smarter Than a Hamster*?"

"Let me check." She looked on the computer. "I'm sorry. We don't. But we have one called *Caring for Your Hamster*."

The librarian was nice. She led them to the shelf where the book was. Jasper, Mom and Dad sat down to read. The book said hamsters liked to eat hamster food. It didn't have any advice on what to do when your hamster is on the loose.

Jasper put his hands over his Band-Aids and
moaned.

"What's wrong, Jasper?" Mom whispered. "Are you
sick?"

"What if Hammy never comes back?"

"Don't worry, son," Dad whispered. "We'll find him."

"What if Nan never comes back!" Jasper wailed.

"She's coming back tomorrow," Mom said in a hushed voice.

"*Tomorrow?*"

"Yes. Tomorrow."

"But we're not finished the cruise ship!"

People were looking at them. Old people frowned and made snapping noises with the newspapers. Kids looked up from their picture books and giggled. Over at the desk, the nice librarian clucked.

"You can work on it this afternoon," Mom said.

"I can't! Ori doesn't want to build it with me anymore!"

Mom put her fingers to Jasper's lips. "Why not?"

Jasper whispered now. He didn't want anybody to hear. "Because I blacked my thumb and waved it in his face and made him sick."

"Why did you do that?"

"Because he was being bossy! He said he was the boss!"

Mom said, "I think Hammy needs a little more time to get back in his cage. Why don't we visit Ori?"

They left the library and got back on their bikes and pedaled over to Ori's house. Mom and Dad waited while Jasper rang the doorbell. When Ori opened the door, Jasper held his two pink thumbs up high so Ori could see them.

Ori smiled.

"I'm sorry I blacked my thumb," Jasper said.

"It's okay," Ori said. "Do you want to work on the ship?"

"It's too late. We'll never finish."

"The thing is," Ori said, "I'll help now."

Jasper said, "I have a better idea. Do you have any paint left?"

Jasper spent the rest of the day at Ori's working on the better idea. Mom and Dad worked in the yard. The three of them stayed out of the house almost the whole day. Then Dad called across the alley and one house down that supper was ready.

"Bad news," he said when Jasper came in the door.

Hammy had eaten all the raisins. He still wasn't in the cage.

That night Jasper made a trail of macaroni to his room. He was so so worried that Hammy wouldn't come back. If he didn't, Jasper would get called to Mrs. Kinoshita's office. He'd probably have to stay in

Mrs. Kinoshita's office for the rest of his life! And what about Nan? He wanted her to come home and see the better idea he and Ori had built. He missed her so so so so much!

"I'm so so so so tired," he told Mom when she came to kiss him good night. "I got so much exercise looking for Hammy and riding bikes to the library and building."

"I know," she said.

"Is Nan really coming home tomorrow?"

"She is."

Before he closed his eyes, he asked, "How long are we going to have to use the toilet paper in the box in the bathroom?"

"A long time," she told him.

"Please," he said. "Never get me my own hamster."

Whirr! Whirr! Whirr!

Whirr! Whirr! Whirr!

Jasper woke in darkness. When he turned on the light, Hammy was sitting on his wheel. He didn't seem too bothered. He just looked at Jasper and wiggled his nose. "Thank you, Hammy," Jasper said.

He got out of bed and closed the door of the cage.

Chapter 12

On Monday morning, Jasper opened his eyes and saw Dad standing in the doorway, smiling. "Will you look at that?" Dad said.

Jasper thought he was talking about Hammy. But he was looking at Jasper's tummy. The covers were down and his pajama top was up. Jasper's tummy looked white as an iceberg and all wrinkly. He couldn't see any holes.

"Did you take off my Band-Aids?" Jasper asked.

"Didn't you?" Dad asked.

They lifted the covers. Thirty-four Band-Aids were stuck on the sheet. They had come off in the night and stuck themselves there like a pancake. Jasper ripped them off. "Look," he said.

Under all the Band-Aids, there was a hole in the sheet.

Then Jasper remembered. He gave a big cheer. "Nan's coming home today!"

After school, Jasper and Mom and Dad picked Nan up at the ship. All three of them fluttered long strips of toilet paper in the air. The toilet paper was Jasper's idea, so they could use up the loose paper in the box faster.

"Nan!" they called as she came down the ramp.

The first thing Nan did was grab Jasper and kiss him seven times, once for each day of the cruise. Jasper could feel the happy lipstick flowers blooming on his cheeks.

Then she held him out so she could look at him. "Jasper? What happened? You look so thin. You look so tired."

"He'll be fine now that you're back," Mom said.

Mom and Dad carried Nan's suitcases. Jasper carried Nan's purse and held her hand. He was never going to let it go. He was going to hold it for the rest of his life. During the drive, neither of them spoke. They sat in the backseat, Jasper sniffing Nan's hand. She smelled the same as ever.

Instead of taking Nan back to her apartment, they brought her to their house where Dad was cooking a special supper. Mom said, "Jasper. Go get Hammy to show Nan."

Jasper was sitting on the sofa with Nan, still holding her hand. "You have to come with me," Jasper told her.

"Nan's tired. Let her rest," Mom said.

"I can't let go of her," Jasper said. "She might get loose again."

Nan said, "I'm not that old. I can get up."

Jasper brought Nan to his room and showed her Hammy in his cage. Nan took a step back. She said, "I'm not that fond of mice."

"It's a hamster," Jasper told her.

Back in the living room, Mom carried in all the yogurt containers on a tray. Nan opened them one by one using the hand Jasper wasn't holding. "What's this?"

"That's the rain you missed."

Nan dipped a finger in the rain. She dabbed some on her wrist and some behind her ears. She opened another yogurt container. "And what's this?"

"That's the air you missed."

Nan put the air on like perfume, too.

"You haven't mentioned the cruise, Nan," Mom said. "Tell us about it."

"Did you see an iceberg?" Jasper asked.

"No! It rained the whole time. Not a single iceberg. Except for iceberg *lettuce!*"

"Yuck!" Jasper said.

"But I met a lot of people, and I played a lot of cards. Except on Wednesday. On Wednesday, I stayed in my cabin and read a book. I told everybody that on Wednesday there was only one person I'd play cards with."

"Me!" Jasper said.

"That's right!" Nan said. "The people were very nice, but they were old. Old people everywhere. I need to be with young people, too."

"I'm young!" Jasper said.

Nan squeezed his hand. "You're my perfect companion. I'm glad I went, but I won't be taking another trip for a long time. Or I'll take you with me."

"Yeah!" Jasper said.

Then Nan said, "Tell me everything that happened to you while I was gone, Jasper."

"Nothing happened."

"Nothing? I don't believe it."

"Jasper!" Dad called from the kitchen. "Things happened!"

"Lots of things," Mom said. "Tell her about your snake story. Tell her about Annie."

"You have to meet Annie," he told Nan. "She has a ring in her nose."

"And you got a mouse," Nan said.

"He's a hamster. And he's not mine. I have to give him back tomorrow."

"Didn't you spend all yesterday afternoon building something for Nan?" Dad called.

Jasper said, "Yes!" He made Nan get up off the sofa again so he could lead her out of the house and all the way across the alley and one house down.

Ori was in the backyard playing on the better idea.

"Oh, Jasper!" Nan cried when she saw it. "You made me an iceberg! How did you do it?"

Jasper told her all about their plan for the cruise ship. "It was as big as an apartment building lying on its side. It was so big it had a swimming pool and a ballroom and a Ping-Pong room. It had ten different restaurants. One only sold popcorn. It even had a back door!"

"I'll show her," Ori said, and he ran into the garage and came back with the plan. Nan unrolled it. She said it looked exactly like the cruise ship she went away on.

"But then we ran out of time because I blacked my thumb and waved it in Ori's face."

"The thing is," Ori said, "I was being bossy."

"So we unnailed the cruise ship and put all the wood back in the pile. Then we painted it white."

"It looks exactly like the icebergs I was supposed to see," Nan told them.

Then Jasper remembered. "Nan! Something did happen when you were gone! Mom tried to eat our jujubes!"

Nan gasped. "She wouldn't!"

"She did!"

Nan pulled her hand out of Jasper's so she could hug him. It was a long, long, long hug that smelled of rain and fresh air.

She said, "Jasper, it's a good thing I'm back."